This Orchard
book belongs to

For Finn.

M.M.

For my mum and best friend –
thanks for EVERYTHING.

J.M.

ORCHARD BOOKS
338 Euston Road
London NW1 3BH
Orchard Books Australia
Level 17/207 Kent Street, Sydney, NSW 2000

First published in 2001 by Orchard Books
First published in paperback in 2002
This edition published in 2012

ISBN 978 1 40831 956 7

A CIP catalogue record for this book is available from the British Library.

1 3 5 7 9 10 8 6 4 2

Printed in China

Orchard Books is a division of Hachette Children's Books,
an Hachette UK company.
www.hachette.co.uk

Wibble Wobble My Loose Tooth

Written by Miriam Moss
Illustrated by Joanna Mockler

ORCHARD

All William ever wanted in the whole world
was to have a **wobbly** tooth.

Everyone else in his class had one.
Louie's twisted round and round
and Rosa's lay flat on its back.

But William's teeth seemed stuck,
superglued to his gums.

"It isn't fair," said William. "Everyone else at school tells *wobbly* tooth stories."

"Sammy swallowed his...

Rosa's fell
down the toilet...

and Louie's flew out
when he scored a goal!"

"When your wobbly tooth comes out, Gran," said William, "you get a silver coin from the Tooth Fairy."

"Is that so?" said Gran.

"Yes," said William. "And if it comes out at school, you have to keep it somewhere safe."

"Vita stuck
hers to the velcro
on her trainers…

and Christie hid his
in the cotton-wool
in his ear.

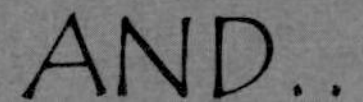

AND…

today Nadir's got lost
up her nose.

Mrs King said she'd keep
them safe from now on."

The next day in quiet time, William felt one of his teeth move at last!

"Mrs King!" he cried. "My tooth moved! I felt it!"

William pushed his tooth forwards with his tongue then sucked it back for Mrs King to see.

"Look, Rosa!" he said.

"Look, Louie!"

"Come on, William," called Mum at bedtime. "How long does it take to brush your teeth?"

"A long time," said William. "It hurts my wobbly tooth."

William just couldn't leave his wobbly tooth alone.

push, pull, jiggle, joggle.
Poke, flick, wibble,
wobble.

"Look, Louie," said William the next day,
twisting his tooth round and round.
"Look, Rosa," he said, as it lay flat on its back.

By bedtime William's tooth was hanging on one thin little thread.

push, pull, jiggle, joggle.
poke, flick, wibble, wobble.

Suddenly, the tooth flipped upside down and got stuck!

"Ow! Ow!" yelled William, jumping out of bed.

"Mum! Dad!" he cried, rushing downstairs.

Gently Dad turned the tooth back the right way up.

"Why doesn't it just come out?" said William.

"Don't worry," said Dad. "It will."

In PE the next day William did his best ever spinning somersault. And when he stood up, his tooth was sitting on his tongue! William took it out and looked at it. How tiny it was!

"Shall I look after it until home time?" asked Mrs King, wrapping it in a tissue and putting it on top of the filing cabinet.

"Then can I take it home?" asked William, feeling a bit wobbly himself.

"Of course you can," said Mrs King.

That afternoon, William sat poking his tongue into the hole in his gum, waiting for Louie to finish vegetable printing.

Suddenly, "Aaargh!" shouted Louie, dancing about. "I've got chilli in my eye!"

"I'll get a tissue, Mrs King," said Rosa.

Mrs King dabbed Louie's eye and before long it was home time.

"Look, Mum!" William said. "My tooth came out!"

"Oh, William!" said Mum. "Can I see it?"

"It's on the filing cabinet, wrapped up in a tissue," said William.

"Here it is," said Mrs King. Then, "Oh! It's gone."

They searched everywhere.
Suddenly William stopped.
"Rosa gave Louie a tissue," he said, "when he got red hot chilli in his eye."
Mum and Mrs King looked at each other.

"Don't worry William," said Mum, searching in the bin. "We'll find it."

William sat down
and stared at his feet.
He was missing his tooth
really badly now.
He was sure they'd
never find it.

Suddenly, Mum stood up. "This might be it!" She unwrapped the tissue – and there was William's tooth!

Mrs King washed the tooth and gave it back to William.

"Perhaps the Tooth Fairy will leave something a bit special tonight," said Mrs King. "After all that."

The next morning William looked under his pillow. There lay a little wooden box. He lifted the lid and inside was a shiny silver coin!

When William got to school he told everyone his **wobbly** tooth story.

"I expect you'd like a rest from **wobbly** teeth for a while, William!" said Mrs King.

"Yes," said William. "I would!"

On the way home from school, William took his silver coin and bought the most enormous ice-cream.

It had little coloured sweets stuck all over it, layers of chocolate, and chewy toffee in the middle.

William unwrapped it and took a big bite.

Ping!

went the little coloured sweets.

Crack!

went the chocolate.

Squelch!

went the ice-cream.

Crunch!

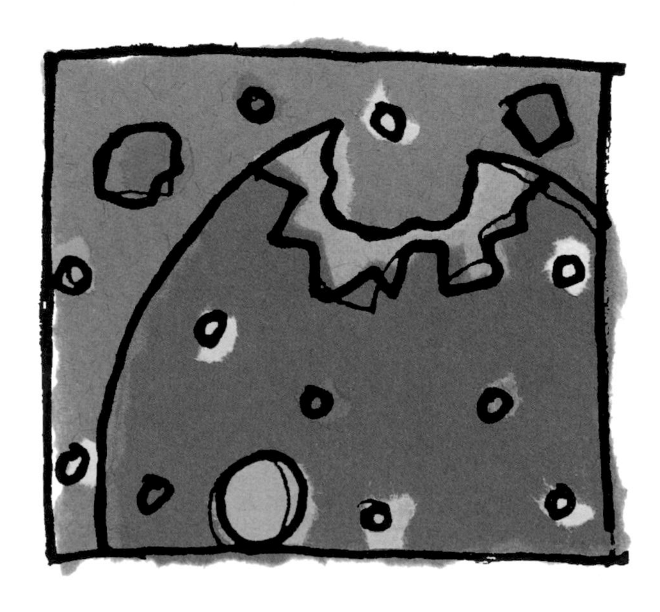

went the ice-cold, rock-hard toffee . . . and guess what?

Another tooth wobbled!

Push, pull, jiggle, joggle.

poke, flick,

wibble,

wobble.